Fire Alert!

Nicholas Allan

RED FOX

A Red Fox Book

Published by Random House Children's Books
20 Vauxhall Bridge Road, London SW1V 2SA

A division of The Random House Group Ltd
London Melbourne Sydney Auckland
Johannesburg and agencies throughout the world

Text © Nicholas Allan 2000
Illustrations © EVA Entertainment Ltd. 2000

1 3 5 7 9 10 8 6 4 2

Printed and bound in Italy by Lego SPA.

THE RANDOM HOUSE GROUP Limited Reg. No. 954009

ISBN 0 09 940786 8

Derek Duck woke early: it was a special day – his plaster cast was coming off.

'You'll soon be flying south with your friends,' said Nurse Kitty, raising the blinds to a blue morning sky – just as a huge crate crashed into the window.

Outside, the Teds, in the ambulance helicopter, were trying to deliver the new supplies.

Dr Matthews waited for the crate to land. 'Now, let's see… seventeen jigsaws… eighty surgical masks… twenty sacks of cotton wool? Four hundred umbrellas?'

He looked up at the window. 'Kitty? Did you order all these?'

'Yes, Dr Matthews. We have to be prepared for every emergency,' she said.

'Of course, Kitty. Just as you say.'

While Ted was busy on his stepladder fixing the window, Surgeon Sally entered the ward with a big pair of scissors. Derek looked worried, but Sally just cut up some cotton wool, which she put into his ears.

Then she brought out an electric saw. It made a terrifying whine.

'Eeek! Ow! Oh!' cried Derek, as she cut into the plaster.

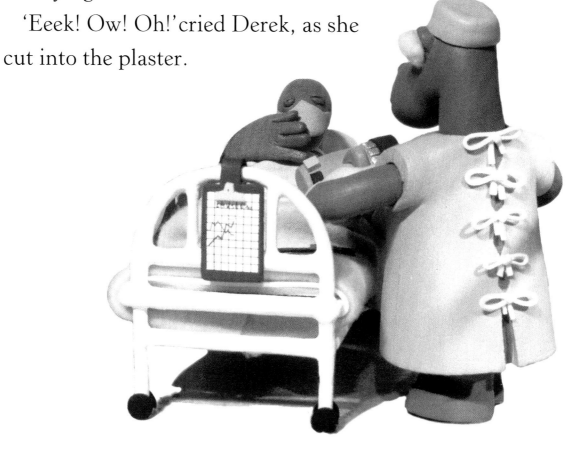

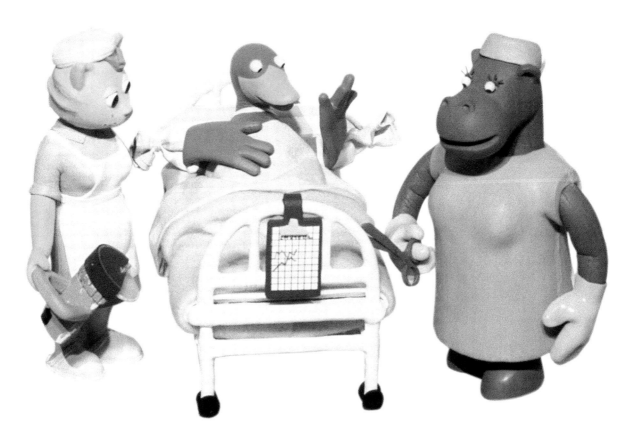

'Don't fuss,' said Sally.

'It's just that… it… tickles!' Derek giggled.

When the cast fell away, Derek's wing looked very thin.

'A little exercise and you'll soon be flying again,' said Sally. 'Take it slowly, one step at a time.'

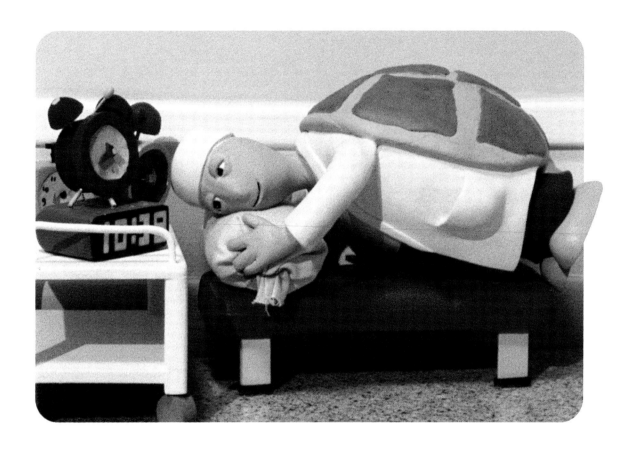

The noise of the saw didn't wake Dr Atticus, but his alarm clock did. He'd been having a short rest before doing his rounds of the ward. As he sat up, he heard music coming from the therapy room: Felicity was trying to help Osbert Owl to sleep.

'You're feeling sleepy… sleepy…' she sang.

Dr Atticus's eyelids grew heavy, and soon he fell back into pleasant dreams.

'Nope,' Osbert said, wide-eyed. 'It's not working. I'm not tired at all.'

Meanwhile, back in the ward, Derek was standing on top of the stepladder.

'Come on! Jump!' cried Ertha Ostrich.

'What d'you know about flying?' said Enrico Elephant in the next bed.

'It's like riding a bike. If you've done it once, you never forget.'

'The way I see it, Derek,' Lana Leopard said, 'all you need is a proper run up…'

Derek, by this time, had lost his balance… and fallen off.

Take a run up, Derek thought later. So he waddled into the corridor.

Kitty was in the corridor, too, pushing a trolley of empty plates. She looked up and saw Derek coming towards her… fast.

Crockery flew, but Derek didn't. Instead, he landed on the trolley, which went clattering down the stairs.

'And when might we possibly need twenty
sacks of cotton wool? Eh, Matthews?' Sally
was saying, as she looked at the new deliveries.
   'Well, Sally, we have to be prepared for
every emergency.'

Just then the trolley and Derek sped past them… and crashed into the sacks of cotton wool.

Watching Derek stand up, unharmed, Sally said, 'Hmm, you may have a point, Dr Matthews.'

'I'm glad you agree, Sally. Now, I'd better unpack these four hundred umbrellas…'

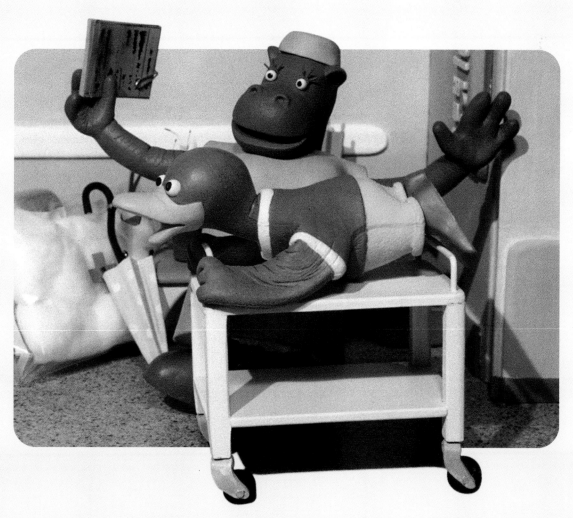

Derek was worried he'd never fly again, so Sally sent him to Felicity, who was good at exercising wings and flippers after an operation. She played soothing music and sang softly: 'It's a beautiful blue sky and you want to fly off into it… Flip two three, flap two three…'

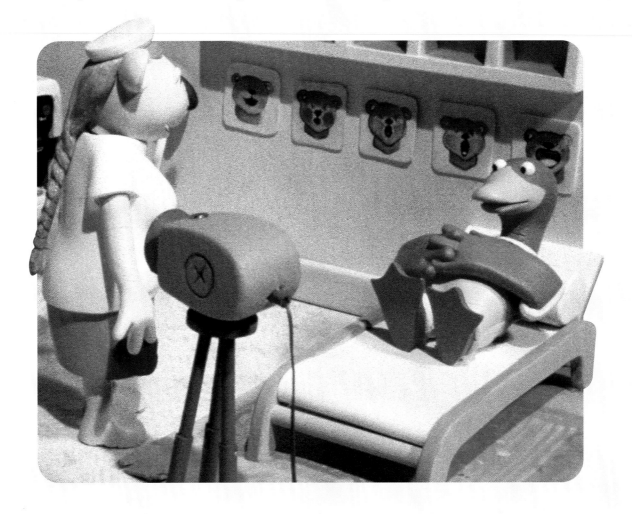

Dr Atticus was walking past
the therapy room.
Hearing the music
and voice, he fell
into a dreamlike
trance, stumbled into
a laundry basket, and
fell asleep.

  'Flip two three, flap
two three,' quacked Derek, happily. He flapped his way
down the ward, making Enrico's newspaper fly up, then
down on to Henry Hedgehog. Henry folded the paper
into a dart and threw it. The dart
flew into the laboratory,
landing on a Bunsen
burner flame...
and that's how the
fire started.

Soon the fire alarm was ringing. Sally handed out cotton wool. 'We don't want to be deafened,' she said.

The clatter of hoofs and claws and flippers sounded, as the patients left the hospital. Outside, a fire engine had arrived. The firebears unrolled the hose and aimed it at the smoke-filled windows.

As the spray fell, Sally passed around umbrellas.
'Umbrellas up!' she ordered.

'Good job we had all those umbrellas,' Kitty
whispered to Dr Matthews.

'Everyone here?' Sally asked.

'I think so, Sally.' Kitty checked. 'Oh dear, there
seems to be a duck and a tortoise missing.'

The ambulance helicopter was flying over the hospital, and the Teds saw Dr Atticus and Derek standing on top of it. When the alarm bell had woken him up, Dr Atticus had hurried up to the roof. Derek had gone after him, thinking he might be able to help.

The Teds tried to fly
closer, but there was
too much smoke.

　'What're we going to do?'
said one Ted.

　'I thought turtles could float,' said the other.

　'In water, stupid, not air. Besides 'e's a tortoise.
There is a difference, Ted.'

　'But ducks can fly, can't they?'

　'Yes… all except that one.'

Dr Atticus and Derek watched the helicopter fly away.

'Now what?' said Dr Atticus.

'I've got an idea,' said Derek suddenly. 'Hold on to me, Dr Atticus... and don't look down.'

Derek stepped over the wall, flapped his wings – and jumped.

''Ere, that duck is flying,' said Ted.

'So's the tortoise.'

'Maybe it's a turtle after all.'

Just then, Dr Atticus fell.

'Maybe not,' said Ted.

The Teds swiftly guided the helicopter towards Dr Atticus, who managed to catch hold of the helicopter ski.

Down below Dr Matthews and Surgeon Sally watched.

'Quickly,' said Sally. 'Pile up those sacks of cotton wool.'

They had just finished, when Dr Atticus fell from the sky and landed on the soft mound.

'There. I knew these sacks of cotton wool would come in handy!' said Sally.

Dr Matthews looked surprised, but before he could
say anything, Derek landed and Kitty
congratulated him. 'Well done,
Derek. You can fly!'

'Well, I had to.'

'Not only that, you're a hero.
Isn't he, Dr Atticus?'

But Dr Atticus, by then,
was fast asleep again.

And after that day, Dr Matthews never again questioned anything Kitty ordered, not even when the Teds arrived in the helicopter with two hundred life-jackets and one hundred sombreros…